George Brown,
CLASS CLOWN

Burp or Treat...
Smell My Feet!

For Amanda, who finds Halloween magical!—NK

For all the fiends that have helped me
celebrate Halloween throughout the years
—AB

GROSSET & DUNLAP
Published by the Penguin Group
Penguin Group (USA) LLC, 375 Hudson Street, New York, New York 10014, USA

USA | Canada | UK | Ireland | Australia | New Zealand | India | South Africa | China

penguin.com
A Penguin Random House Company

Text copyright © 2014 by Nancy Krulik. Illustrations copyright © 2014 by Aaron Blecha. All rights reserved. Published by Grosset & Dunlap, a division of Penguin Young Readers Group, 345 Hudson Street, New York, New York 10014. GROSSET & DUNLAP is a trademark of Penguin Group (USA) LLC. Printed in the USA.

Library of Congress Cataloging-in-Publication Data is available.

ISBN 978-0-448-46115-1   10 9 8 7 6 5 4 3 2 1

George Brown, CLASS CLOWN

Burp or Treat... Smell My Feet!

by Nancy Krulik
illustrated by Aaron Blecha

Grosset & Dunlap
An Imprint of Penguin Group (USA) LLC

Chapter 1

"Get the full-size candy bars, Mom," George Brown pleaded. "Kids hate when you give them the mini fun-size ones."

George's mom looked at the stacks and stacks of bags of Halloween candy on the store shelf. "Nope, sorry. It's the mini candy bars, or no candy bars."

"At least your mom gives away candy on Halloween," George's best friend, Alex, said. "My mom gives everyone **mini tubes of toothpaste**. Talk about embarrassing."

George gave Alex a sympathetic look. "I guess that's what happens when your mom is a dentist."

Alex nodded and pointed to the

shelves filled with **ooey, gooey** sugary candy. "This place is my mom's worst nightmare. She calls candy bars a cavity waiting to happen."

"Which is why it's good you boys will get toothpaste in your trick-or-treat bags," George's mom interrupted. She gave George a stern look. "And you really have to watch how much you eat in one sitting. **Remember what happened last year.**"

"Don't remind me," George said with a groan. This Halloween, he would try not to eat his whole bag of candy in one night. But then again, he made that same promise every year.

"I still have a few things to buy," George's mom told the boys. "Why don't you two go over to the next aisle and take a look at the masks?"

"Good idea!" George shouted.

"Right behind you, dude," Alex said as he followed him to the costume aisle.

Alex picked up a **clown costume** in a box. "I remember when I used to wear these kinds of costumes," he said. "I hated the plastic masks with the rubber band around the back."

"Me too," George agreed. "I could never see through the eyeholes, and it got all hot and sweaty near where my nose was supposed to go."

Alex walked farther down the aisle and picked up a **rubber monster mask**. "Now *this* is cool," he said.

George looked at the mask. It had rubber nails jammed into the neck, big **bulging eyes**, and blood dripping down the sides. It was scary.

But not nearly as scary as what was suddenly happening in the bottom of George's belly. There was something *really* frightening going on down there. **Bubbles.** Hundreds of them. And they were bouncing around madly.

Bing-bang. Ping-pang.

George gulped. Those weren't ordinary, weak, wimpy bubbles. They were strong, crazy bubbles. Bubbles that kickboxed his kidneys and boomeranged from his bladder. Bubbles that were threatening to burst out of him **at any moment**, and . . .

Just then, George let out a powerful burp. **A super burp.** A burp so loud, and so strong, it knocked the rubber mask right out of Alex's hands.

"Dude! No!" Alex shouted.

Dude! Yes! The magical super burp had escaped. And now, whatever the burp wanted to do, George had to do.

The burp wanted to eat some candy corn. So the next thing George knew, his feet were running back over to the candy aisle. His hands reached out, grabbed a big bag of candy corn, ripped it open, and started pouring the orange-and-yellow candies into his mouth.

"Kid, what are you doing?" one of the store's employees shouted at him.

Then he called across the store to George's mom. "Lady, is this your kid?"

George's mother turned around. "Oh no. Not again!" she cried out. Her cheeks got all red. "George! Stop that right now!"

George wanted to stop. He really did. He didn't even like candy corn. But the super burp *loved* candy corn.

"Lady, you're going to have to pay for that candy," the employee said.

"George, get out of the candy aisle this instant!" his mother yelled.

For once, the burp let George do what he was told. George bolted back toward the costume aisle.

A few older girls were standing there, buying face paint. George pushed them aside and grabbed a green rubber mask with bulging eyes and snakes for hair.

"Can't you say excuse me?" one of the girls demanded.

George wanted to say excuse me. **But he couldn't.** The burp never said excuse me for anything.

Instead, George threw on the mask and started shaking his head. The rubbery snakes wiggled all around.

"Hiss! Hiss!" George's mouth said.

One of the older girls shuddered. "I

hate snakes," she told her friend. "Even fake ones."

"Snakeman **bites**!" George said.

The girls grabbed packets of face paint and hurried out of the aisle.

George's mother came running over. "Put that mask back on the shelf. NOW!"

George stared at his mom. Her face had gone from red to purple. She looked like her head might **explode**.

"And tie your shoelace," George's mom continued. "You're going to fall."

"Hissssss!" George replied.

A little boy who had been looking at a Superman costume **started to cry**. "SNAKES! That monster's scary!"

The boy's mother turned to George's mom. "You need to control your son!" she told her.

"George!" his mother shouted. "NO MORE WARNINGS. Stop what you're

doing this instant." She reached out and
tried to grab him. But George was fast. He
began to run down the aisle.

"Hisssss!"

Whoops!

Plop.

George tripped over his shoelace and
landed on his belly. Quickly, he flipped
over onto his back. His arms and legs

waved crazily in the air. He looked like **an upside-down crab**. Well, an upside-down crab with a scary snake-haired mask on its head.

George yanked off his sneakers and waved his stinky feet in the air. **"Trick or treat! Smell my feet!"** he shouted.

The little boy cried harder.

The smell of **stinky feet** spread through the store.

Pop! Just then George felt something burst in the bottom of his belly. All the air rushed out of him. The super burp was gone.

But George was still there, with the mask on his head, and his feet in the air. Quickly he sat up, whipped off the mask, and looked around. **No one looked happy.** Even Alex was shaking his head.

"Dude, your feet **smell**," Alex said.

George opened his mouth to say, "I'm sorry." And that's exactly what came out.

"George, get up," his mom demanded. "And put your shoes back on. We're going home. We'll talk about this later."

George frowned. He was in trouble. Again.

Stupid super burp. It was all tricks and no treat.

Chapter 2

"How much trouble are you in?" Alex asked George over the phone **later that afternoon**.

"My mom's pretty angry," George admitted. "I had to pay her back for the candy I ate at the store. And then she made me clean out the garage as a **punishment**. Not exactly the way I wanted to spend Sunday afternoon."

"It could have been worse," Alex pointed out. "The burp really made you go out of control."

"I hate burps," George **groaned**. "More than anything."

"I know," Alex said, trying to sound

as if he understood. But how could he? George was the only kid in town who was bugged by burps. Oh sure, other kids burped sometimes. But nobody burped quite the way George did.

It all started when George and his family first arrived in Beaver Brook. George's dad was in the army, so the family moved around a lot. George knew that first days at school could be **pretty rotten**. But *this* first day was the most rotten.

In his old school, George had been the class clown. He was always pulling pranks and making jokes. But George had promised himself that things were going to be different at Edith B. Sugarman Elementary School. He was turning over a new leaf. **No more pranks.** No more whoopee cushions or spitballs shot through straws. No more bunny ears behind people's heads. No more goofing on teachers when their backs were turned.

Of course, being the non-funny new kid in school didn't exactly make him popular. And as he left school that first day, the only friend George had was the same one he walked in with: Me, myself, and I.

That night, George's parents took him out to Ernie's Ice Cream Emporium. While they were sitting outside and George was finishing his root beer float, **a shooting star** flashed across the sky. So George made a wish.

I want to make kids laugh—but not get into trouble.

Unfortunately, the star was gone before George could finish the wish. So only half came true—**the first half**.

A minute later, George had a funny feeling in his belly. It was like there were hundreds of tiny bubbles **bouncing** around in there. The bubbles hopped up and down and all around. They ping-ponged their way into his chest, and bing-bonged their way up into his throat. And then . . .

George let out a big burp. A *huge* burp. A SUPER burp!

The super burp was loud, and it was *magic*.

Suddenly George lost control of his arms and legs. It was like they had minds of their own. His hands grabbed straws and stuck them up his nose like a walrus. His feet jumped up on the table and started dancing the **hokey pokey**. Everyone at Ernie's Emporium started laughing—except George's parents, who were covered in the ice cream he'd kicked over while he was dancing.

That wasn't the only time the burp burst out of George. There had been plenty of major gas attacks since then. And every time the burp burst out of him, it made George do terrible things. Like **juggle raw eggs** in the middle of the classroom—which would have been fine if George knew how to juggle.

Or jump so high on a trampoline that his **tighty whities** got caught on a tree branch on the way down. Talk about getting the world's worst wedgie. Ouch!

And then there was the time the super

burp made George tickle Louie Farley's underarms during a lice check.

That had been horrible. Louie was George's worst enemy, and he had really **stinky pits**. George wound up with smelly Louie sweat all over his fingers. Yuck! George never told anyone about the super burp. He figured they'd never believe him.

George wouldn't have believed it, either, if he weren't the one it kept happening to.

But Alex was smart. He had figured out George's **secret**. Luckily, Alex was a good friend. He hadn't told anyone about the magical super burp. And he'd volunteered to help George find a cure. So far nothing they'd tried had squelched the belch, but the boys weren't giving up.

"Have you found any new **burping cures?**" George whispered into the phone.

"Not yet. But I'm working on it," Alex assured him. "I've been reading the Burp No More Blog every day. And the new issue of my science magazine should be coming in the mail soon. There could be something in there."

"I sure hope so," George said. "Because this burp attack was really bad. I was afraid my mom was going to **ground** me, and I'd miss Halloween."

"I'm glad she didn't," Alex said.

"I know. I can't wait for Halloween!" George exclaimed.

As George hung up the phone, he hoped he'd be able to trick his burp into staying out of sight. Otherwise, Halloween would go from fun to not so much . . .

HALLOWEEN PARADE THIS THURSDAY!

The orange-and-black banner was the first thing George saw as he and his friends walked into the school building Monday morning.

"We're having a parade?" he asked Alex. "With floats and everything?"

Alex shook his head. "Not exactly. It's just everyone marching around the playground. We do it every year."

"Oh," George said quietly. That didn't sound very exciting.

"It's a lot of fun," George's friend Julianna said. "Everyone comes in **costume**, and there's music and candy."

21

"We don't have classes the whole afternoon," Chris pointed out. "And **no homework** that night."

"Oh," George said again, with a smile. This time he sounded more excited. And also a little confused. He was doing some math in his head, and the numbers **didn't add up**. "But Halloween won't come for, like, a week and a half after that parade."

"It's Principal McKeon's way of psyching everyone up for Halloween," Alex explained.

That **surprised** George. He never thought of Principal McKeon as the kind of person who would want to psych kids up for Halloween. She only got excited about learning stuff. And Halloween wasn't supposed to be about learning. It was supposed to be fun!

"What are you going to be for Halloween, Georgie?" Sage asked. Then she did that **weird eyelash-blinking thing** she always did when she was talking to him.

BLINK
BLINK
BLINK

George hated the eyelash thing. He didn't like being called Georgie, either. "I don't know yet," he mumbled.

"Maybe we could do something together," Sage suggested. "Like I could be Cinderella and you could be **Prince Charming**."

George shook his head. Uh-uh. Not happening. "I'm probably going to be something scary," he told her.

"You mean like Frankenstein?" Sage asked.

George nodded.

"Then I could be the *Bride* of Frankenstein," Sage **squealed** happily.

George frowned. That was *not* what he had in mind.

Just then, Louie zoomed by on his wheelie sneakers. **"Out of my way!"** he shouted.

"Why are you in such a hurry to get to class?" George asked him.

"I'm practicing leading the crowd," Louie said.

"For what?" George wondered.

ZOOM!

"For when I'm chosen to lead the Halloween parade," Louie replied. "The kid who has the **best costume** always leads the parade."

"It's not the best costume," Julianna corrected him. "It's the most *creative* costume."

"My school costume will be the best— and most creative," Louie assured her.

"Your *school* costume?" George asked.

"Sure," Louie said boastfully. "I always have two costumes. One for school and one for the actual night of Halloween. And they're both always **amazing**."

"That's true," Louie's friend Max agreed. "Always."

"Amazing," Louie's other friend, Mike, added.

Wow. Two costumes. George had to admit that was impressive. But not surprising. Louie always seemed to have

twice as much of everything.

"I'll see you guys after school," Chris said as he turned the corner and walked into his classroom.

"Later," George said. He headed toward his classroom, but stopped short at the doorway. Everyone did.

"What's going on?" Alex asked.

George couldn't believe what he was seeing. Someone had **flipped all the desks** upside down. The chairs, too. The drawers of the filing cabinet had been pulled open, and some of the books had been taken off the shelves and thrown onto the floor.

George's teacher, Mrs. Kelly, was standing in the middle of the room, staring at the mess.

"Maybe it's some sort of Halloween

prank," George suggested.

"Pranks are for April Fools' Day,"
Louie told him. "Not Halloween."

"Okay, then *you* explain it," George
replied.

"No problem," Max said. "Louie can
explain it."

"Louie's great at explaining," Mike
agreed. "He can explain anything."

But Louie couldn't explain *this*.

"If it is a prank, I don't think it's very
funny," Mrs. Kelly said. "It's going to
take us a lot of time to put this room back
together. And that's a shame, because I
had something **really special** planned for
this morning."

George wasn't sure how he felt about
that. Mrs. Kelly's idea of "something
special" wasn't always his idea of
something special.

Still, cleaning the classroom **wasn't**

going to be fun. But they had to do it. First, the kids flipped their desks right-side up. Then they worked to put the books back on the shelves while Mrs. Kelly fixed up her filing cabinet.

As they were putting the last book away, Julianna found a note. But the note wasn't handwritten. It was made of letters cut from newspapers and magazines.

Julianna read the note out loud.

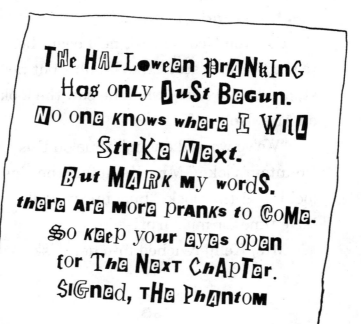

THe HALLoween pRANkInG
Has onLy JuSt BeGun.
No one knows where I WILL
StriKe Next.
But MARk my wordS.
there Are more pranks to CoMe.
So keep your eyes open
for THe Next ChApTer.
SiGned, tHe PhAntoM

"The Phantom?" Alex wondered out loud. "Who's that?"

"Could be anyone," George said.

"And what does he mean, 'keep your eyes open'?" Louie asked.

"I don't know," Mrs. Kelly said. "What do you think it means?"

"Maybe he means don't fall asleep in school," Mike said.

"I fell asleep once in the cafeteria," Max said. "My face landed right in my **meatballs and spaghetti**."

Boy, did George wish he'd been there to see that. He started to laugh—but he stopped right away when he saw the look on Mrs. Kelly's face.

"We've wasted enough time on this Phantom's joke," Mrs. Kelly told the class, looking at the clock. "Luckily, we still have time for my surprise."

Mrs. Kelly reached into her desk

drawer and pulled out her iPod. She plugged it into a speaker, and began to play music.

"The toe bone's connected to the foot bone, the foot bone's connected to the ankle bone . . . ," Mrs. Kelly **sang along** with the music. She wiggled her foot all around. "Come on, you guys. Get up and do the Halloween Skeleton Dance!"

George didn't want to dance. Not at all. But Mrs. Kelly took her dancing seriously. She'd be angry if he didn't get up and **start dancing**. So he got out of his seat and joined the rest of the class in the Halloween Skeleton Dance.

"The ankle bone's connected to the leg bone," Mrs. Kelly sang out. "Now shake those **skeleton bones**!" Mrs. Kelly began to shake all over. So did most of the kids.

But not George. He wasn't listening to the music anymore. **He couldn't.** The only

thing George could pay attention to was
the bubbles that were suddenly dancing
up and down inside his belly.

The super burp was back! Already

the bubbles were hip-hopping on his hip bone, and bouncing off his backbone.

Oh no! If the super burp burst out now, there was no telling what it might do.

George had to **squelch that belch**. But . . . how?

"The knee bone's connected to the thigh bone," Mrs. Kelly sang out.

Plink-plonk. Zink-zonk. The bubbles were moving faster now. They were ricocheting off his ribs and trekking up his trachea. George had to stop them **before they made it to his mouth**.

There was only one thing to do. George was going to have to trick those bubbles into moving back down toward his toes. Quickly, he flipped over, and did **a handstand**.

"Look! George's acting all weird!" Louie shouted.

The kids all turned to stare at George. But he didn't care. All George knew was that it was working. The bubbles were still moving up, up, up. But now **up was down**. The bubbles moved past George's neck bone, which connected to his collarbone. Then they moved to his rib bones, which connected to his backbone, which . . .

Pop! Suddenly, George felt something burst in his belly. All the air rushed right

out of him. The super burp was gone.

But George was still there. Standing upside down.

Mrs. Kelly frowned at George.

Uh-oh. This was *ba-a-ad*.

Or maybe not. George was upside down. So what looked like a frown was actually a smile. Mrs. Kelly was *smiling* at George.

"Excellent, George," Mrs. Kelly said. "I love your **interpretive dancing**. And you're right: No matter which way we stand, our bones are still connected! Now come on everybody, shake those bones."

The kids all began to shake.

George glanced over at Louie. He was looking at George and smiling. Well, not really. George was looking at Louie upside down. So his smile was really a frown. Louie hated when anyone got a compliment—**other than himself**, of course.

Louie's frown made George smile. He'd managed to squelch the belch *and* make Louie miserable. It didn't get much better than that.

Chapter 4

"Oh yeah!" George cheered as he and Alex left the lunch line with their trays and headed toward the fourth-grade table. "Spaghetti and meatballs for lunch. This day just keeps getting **better and better**."

"It's definitely the best hot lunch they serve," Alex agreed.

George plopped his tray down on the table next to Julianna and Alex, and across from Louie, Max, and Mike. The smell of meatballs and tomato sauce **floated** up to George's nose. And then . . . suddenly . . . his stomach started to rumble.

George gulped. Uh-oh. Not again.

Grumble rumble.

Rumble grumble.

Phew! That wasn't a bubbling sound. That was a hungry belly sound. And it was *easy* to squelch. All George had to do was take a **big bite** of a meatball.

"Aaaaahhhhh!"

Before George could even take one bite of his lunch, he heard Sage **scream**. He turned just in time to see her drop her tray.

Crash! Meatballs and spaghetti flew all over the place. A few kids clapped.

"WORM!" Sage shouted. She ran over to the table and grabbed George's shirt. "Help me, Georgie!" she begged.

George quickly pried himself away from Sage. "Get off of me," he told her. "What's wrong with you?"

"Th-there's a **worm** in my food!" Sage told him. "I hate worms. They're so *slimy*."

Quickly, the kids in the lunchroom gathered around to see what was happening.

George looked down at the pile of spaghetti and meatball mess on the floor. Sure enough, there was something **gray and slimy-looking** mixed in with the spaghetti. He reached down and picked it up.

"You're scared of this?" he asked, waving the worm in front of Sage's nose.

"Ooo. Get that away from me, Georgie," she squealed.

"It's rubber," George told her. "Someone was just pulling a prank on you."

A few kids laughed.

"Oh," Sage said, **embarrassed**. "I thought it was real."

"It *looks* real," Julianna agreed.

"Until you look at it closely," Alex commented. "Then you see it doesn't have any parapodia."

George stared at Alex. "Para-whatia?"

"Parapodia," Alex repeated. **"Tiny hair-like things** that help the worm move. I read about them in a science book once. That worm doesn't have them."

Just then, Mr. Coleman, the school janitor, came over with a mop and started to clear away Sage's spilled food. He didn't look happy. "First someone uses tape to post a note on my freshly painted cafeteria wall, and now this," he grumbled.

"There was a note?" George asked him.

"What did it say?" Louie wondered.

Mr. Coleman reached into his pocket and pulled out a piece of paper **covered in letters** cut from magazines and newspapers. He read the note out loud. "'Always check the contents of your food before you eat. Signed, The Phantom.'

"I have no idea what it means," Mr. Coleman said with a shrug. He shoved the note back in his pocket and went back to mopping the floor.

The kids looked at one another. They knew what the note meant. They just didn't know why this Phantom guy was leaving notes for them.

Just then, Principal McKeon walked over to the lunch table and frowned. **"What's going on here?"** she asked.

Sage pointed to the rubber worm in George's hand. "I thought it was a real worm," she told Principal McKeon. "Georgie was so brave. He reached right into the hot spaghetti and pulled it out."

"It was just rubber," George told her.

"But you didn't know that," Sage insisted.

"Or did he?" Louie asked.

George gave Louie a **funny look**. Louie glared back at him.

"Sage, please help Mr. Coleman pick

up the plate and silverware," Principal McKeon said. "Then you may go get another lunch."

"Yes, ma'am," Sage said. She bent down and started to **clean up** the mess.

Principal McKeon shook her head. "Pranks are not funny," she said as she glanced up at the black-and-orange Halloween parade banner hanging from the rafters. "You students have a lot of privileges in our school. **Privileges can easily be taken away.**" And with that, she walked out of the cafeteria.

No one said anything for a minute. Finally, George turned to Louie. "Why did you make it sound like I already knew the worm was rubber?" he demanded.

"What do you mean?" Louie asked him.

"You know," George insisted. "When Sage told everyone I didn't know the worm was rubber, you said 'Or did he?'

right in front of the principal."

"Well, you sure grabbed that worm fast," Louie explained. "And you weren't scared at all. So you must have **known it was fake**. Only you couldn't have known it was fake . . . *unless you were the one who put it there.*"

"You think *I* pulled that prank on Sage?" George asked.

"It's the kind of thing you would do," Louie told him. "You're always **joking around**. And Sage is always driving you crazy . . . *Georgie.*"

Max and Mike both started to laugh.

Grrrr. It was bad enough when Sage called him that.

"I'm just **not afraid** of worms," George said. "I'd have picked it up even if it was a real one."

"Sure," Louie said. "Whatever you say."

"Yeah, sure," Max agreed.

"Sure, sure," Mike added.

George couldn't believe Louie was accusing him of being **the prankster**. Okay, at his old school, George played pranks on kids every once in a while. Like when he pretended to take a picture of his pal Katie Kazoo with a camera that squirted water, or put a whoopee cushion on the seat of snooty Suzanne Lock in the school cafeteria. **But George didn't do stuff like that anymore.**

Besides, there was something else Louie hadn't considered. "When would I have dropped the worm in Sage's food? I came in the cafeteria the same time you did. And I was sitting right here with you when she saw it for the first time."

Louie didn't answer. He couldn't argue with that. "I don't know how you did it," he told George. "But I do know Principal McKeon was staring right at that parade banner when she talked about taking away privileges. And I am *not* going to let that parade **be canceled**. Not when I'm going to be this year's leader. So you just better cut it out, George."

George didn't answer. Instead he

picked up his fork and started to roll his spaghetti around and around. Only he wasn't very hungry anymore.

Louie was right. Mrs. McKeon had been looking at that banner. Everyone knew it. Even George's friends. They were all very quiet. George could tell they were worried the parade would be canceled. And he was even *more* worried that they would **blame him** if it was.

So much for this day getting better and better. Thanks to Louie and the Phantom, spaghetti and meatballs day was ruined.

Chapter 5

"So, have you guys decided what you're going to dress up as for the Halloween parade?" Chris asked Alex and George as the boys met up on the playground before school the next morning.

George shook his head. "Not yet. This has to be an extra-special costume. It's my **first parade**."

"True," Alex agreed. "The rest of us have been doing this since kindergarten."

"But it's still special," Chris said. "That's why **I'm going to be Toiletman!**"

George laughed. Toiletman was a

cartoon superhero Chris had created. Whenever there was a chance to dress up— for the school talent show or a Halloween parade—Chris put on his Toiletman cape.

"My mom said I could buy a **new plunger**, so I'm really psyched!" Chris added. "And I know that no one else is coming dressed as Toiletman."

"That's for sure," George said.

"I'm thinking of coming as Sir Alexander Fleming," Alex told Chris and George.

George looked at him curiously. "Who?"

"Sir Alexander Fleming," Alex repeated, sounding kind of surprised that George didn't know who he was talking about. "He was a scientist who worked with **mold and bacteria**. He discovered penicillin."

"Oh," George said. "Well, mold's kind of cool."

"Mold's *very* cool," Alex corrected him.

"I bet no one else will have that costume, either," Chris said.

The pressure was really on George now. He had to come up with an original costume idea. But what?

Rrrinnngggg. Just then, the bell rang. It was time to go inside. School was starting. Halloween was going to have to wait.

"What's going on?" George wondered as he and his friends walked into the school building. It looked like **every kid** in the school was in the lobby.

"I don't know," Alex said. "But something definitely has to be going on."

"Whoa," George heard someone in the crowd gasp.

"Principal McKeon's going to have a fit," someone else added.

George just had to know what was happening! He **squeezed** himself through the crowd of kids that had gathered in the middle of the school lobby.

"Oh man, check out Edith B.!" George laughed so hard, **he snorted**. Someone had put fake eyeglasses, a rubber nose, and a mustache on the sculpture of Edith B. Sugarman. The school was named for Edith B. Sugarman—although no one seemed to know who she was or why anyone would name a school after her. The sculpture was **pretty weird looking** to begin with. But now it looked hilarious.

Alex started to laugh, too. So did Chris. And Julianna. And even Louie. Before long, everyone was hysterical.

Well, *almost* everyone.

"You think this is funny?" Principal McKeon bellowed from behind the crowd. "Well, I

don't. I demand to know who did this."

"There's a note on the bottom of the statue," Louie pointed out.

Principal McKeon grabbed the note and began to read it out loud. "'I cover my tracks well. You will never find the Phantom.'"

"AAAAAHHHHH!"

Just as Principal McKeon finished reading, a scream came from Nurse Cuttaway's office.

Uh-oh. What now? George looked at Alex.

Alex looked back at George and shrugged.

There was only one way to find out. The boys raced toward the nurse's office. The rest of the kids headed that way, too.

"Oh wow!" George peeked into the nurse's office and tried not to laugh. But holding in giggles was almost as hard as holding in burps. "Hahahahahha!"

George wasn't the only one laughing. It was hard *not* to laugh at a life-size bony skeleton with a green rubber monster mask over its head. The mask had bulging eyes and snakes for hair.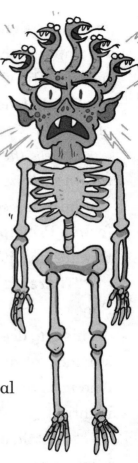

"Hey, George, isn't that the same mask that you . . . ," Alex began.

But before Alex could finish his sentence, Principal McKeon walked over and **yanked** the mask off the skeleton's head.

"Who did this?" she demanded, waving the rubber mask in the air. The rubbery snakes wiggled and jiggled. "This skeleton belongs in the science room," Principal McKeon continued. "Not in the nurse's office."

Clunk. One of the skeleton's feet fell off.

I guess the foot bone's not connected to the ankle bone anymore, George thought. But he didn't say that out loud. He had a feeling Principal McKeon wouldn't find that funny, either.

"There's a note near the skeleton," Sage said. She began to read it out loud. " 'This guy doesn't have a brain, a heart, a stomach, or an appendix. He's got no *body*. And *nobody* can guess the Phantom's true identity!' "

"As I told a group of you yesterday, I am prepared to **take away** some very important privileges if this prankster is not stopped immediately," Principal McKeon said to the crowd gathered outside the nurse's office. "There have to be **consequences** for someone's actions."

George frowned as he noticed the principal's eyes drifting toward the Halloween parade banner in the front hallway of the school. He knew what she meant. And he bet the other kids did, too.

"George, you better **cut it out**," Louie said as the kids started moving down the hall to their classrooms.

"Me?" George asked. "I didn't do anything."

"Yeah, right," Louie said. "These are just the kind of weird, freaky jokes a **weirdo freak** like you would play. If Mrs. McKeon cancels that parade, it's gonna be your fault."

Louie said that last part really loud. A bunch of kids in the hall turned and stared at George.

George shook his head. **"It wasn't me,"**

he repeated. "I'm not the Phantom."

The kids kept staring. Some of them were *glaring*. Louie was the only one smiling. Louie was never happier than when he was **causing trouble** for someone else—especially for George.

Chapter 6

"There he is," George heard a third-grader whisper to his friend in the lunch line later that day. **The kid pointed to George.** "The one who's going to ruin everything."

"I hear he's new here. He probably didn't have a Halloween parade at his old school," the other third-grader said.

"He must really hate Halloween. Or parades."

George's face turned **bright red**. That wasn't true at all. George *loved* Halloween. And parades.

"You guys know it wasn't me," George said to Chris, Alex, and Julianna as they

sat down at the lunch table.

"I believe you," Julianna said.

"Me too," Alex said. "It was just weird that the skeleton in the nurse's office was wearing the same mask you tried on in the store the other day. Good thing you were **kicked out** before you could buy the mask. Because if you hadn't been . . ."

"That would have been another clue that pointed to me," George finished.

Just then two fifth-graders walked past George and his friends.

"Jerk," one of them said, coughing into his hand as he passed.

"If Principal McKeon really does cancel the parade, everyone will think it's my fault," George **groaned**.

"I know how to stop that from happening," Chris said suddenly.

"How?" George asked.

"Easy," Chris said. "We just have to

find out who the real Phantom is, and tell him to **stop pranking**."

"How?" George repeated.

Chris shrugged. "I didn't figure that part out yet."

There was something else that no one had figured out yet—how to stop the super burp from bursting out of George. That was a solution George could have really used. **Right now!** Because the bubbles were back.

Bing-bong. Ping-pong. The bubbles bounced on George's bladder, and leaped onto his lungs. They jumped up to George's jaw and tickled his tongue.

George shut his mouth tight and tried to trap the burp. But the bubbles were strong. Too strong.

Suddenly George let out a burp. It wasn't a supersonic super burp. It was more like a mini burp. But that was enough.

His hands grabbed a big slice of **salami** from his tray and slapped it against his face like a mask. George's nose poked itself right through the slice of salami.

Aachooo! George's nose **sneezed**!

"Gross!" Louie yelled.

"Oh, Georgie!" Sage gasped. "You're not going to eat that now, are you?"

George wanted to tell Sage he didn't eat **booger-covered salami**. But when he opened his mouth, all that came out was, "Not without mustard!"

George's hand folded itself into a fist and slammed down on one of the mustard packs on his tray.

Squirt! Mustard flew up in the air.

"Cut that out!" Louie shouted from across the table. "I don't like mustard."

HEEEYAH!

"Mount Mustard is erupting!" George shouted. He popped three mustard packs with one big blow. "Take cover!"

Sage moved her chair away. "This is my favorite shirt, Georgie," she told him. "Don't get mustard on it, please!"

"Whoa!" Chris exclaimed as he watched a **big glob** of mustard shoot into the air. "I think you just got mustard on the ceiling. *Impressive*."

"Dude, you gotta stop," Alex told him. "Principal McKeon's on her way over."

But George couldn't stop. He wasn't in charge anymore. **The super burp was.**

George grabbed two packs of mustard from Chris's tray. He pulled his fist back, and got ready to **pound**. And then . . .

Pop! George felt the air rush right out of him. The mini super burp was gone. But George was still there. With salami on his face and mustard on his fist.

"George Brown! **What are you doing?**" Principal McKeon demanded. "Food is not meant to be played with."

George opened his mouth to say, "I'm sorry." And that's exactly what came out.

"Get some napkins and clean up this mess," the principal told him.

As the principal walked away, Louie shook his head. "First you pull all your

Phantom pranks, and now you're making mustard **explode**. You won't stop until the principal is so mad she cancels the parade!"

By now, half the kids in the cafeteria were staring at George.

George frowned. **"Stick a fork in me,"** he groaned to Alex, Julianna, and Chris. "I'm done."

"Don't worry, dude," Alex assured him. "We'll figure something out."

George knew Alex was trying to be nice. But Alex had been trying for months to solve George's burp problem. And that thing was **still around**.

The parade was scheduled for the day after tomorrow. If they didn't find the **true identity** of the Phantom soon, George wasn't going to need a Halloween costume. He could just go as George Brown, world's most hated fourth-grader.

Chapter 7

"I love art class, don't you, *Georgie?*"
Sage asked George later that afternoon as
Mrs. Kelly's class walked down the hall to
the art room.

George **shrugged**. "Sure," he told her.
"Art's cool."

"We're painting self-portraits today,"
Sage continued. "That's why I wore **my
favorite shirt**. Because I always want to
remember how much I loved this shirt.
And with a painting . . ."

George kept looking at Sage, even
though he really wasn't listening anymore.
He was just watching her mouth move up
and down. It was kind of amazing how

much Sage could talk once she got going.
Blah, blah, blah . . .

Whoops! Bam!

The next thing George knew, he was sitting on the floor.

Well, actually, **he was sitting on top of Louie**, who was lying on the floor because George had just **slammed** into him.

"What are you doing?" Louie demanded.

"Walking to art class," George answered. "At least I was until I bumped into you. Why did you stop?"

"To pick up this quarter," Louie explained. **"But it's stuck to the floor."**

George reached over and tried to pick up the quarter. Sure enough, it was glued down. George took another look.

"I can't believe you fell for that," George said with a laugh. "It's one of the **oldest gags** in the world."

"You *know* it's a gag?" Louie asked him.

"Well, yeah," George said. "Look. The coin says, United *Snakes* of America. Real quarters don't say that."

"So you admit this glued quarter was **a prank**," Louie continued.

"Of course it is," George said.

"That proves it," Louie announced.

"Proves what?" George asked.

"Only the Phantom would know it was a prank," Louie pointed out proudly—and loudly.

"Anyone would have known it was **a fake**," George insisted. "Just look at it. Don't you see . . ."

But Louie wasn't listening to George anymore. Louie was too busy listening to Max and Mike, who were telling him how wonderful he was. Again.

"You're a genius," Max complimented Louie.

"You definitely proved it," Mike agreed.

George looked around. Some of the other kids in the hallway were whispering to each other. Even Alex and Julianna were **looking at him strangely**.

George couldn't believe it. Was it

possible that his best friends doubted him,
too? Why? It was obvious Louie hadn't
really **proved anything**—except that he
was a total jerk. And everybody already
knew *that*.

"The Phantom's note from the quarter
was actually pretty **creepy**," Alex told
Chris at the end of the day. "It said,
'Paging all kids! Your days are numbered—
not much time to find the Phantom.'"

"You remembered **the whole note** by
heart?" Chris asked him.

"It was too creepy to forget." Alex said.

"Where was it posted?" Chris asked.

"On the wall near the fake quarter Louie tried to pick up," Julianna said.

"The quarter Louie accused *me* of gluing to the floor," George added. "When would I have time to do that? I was with the class the **whole day**." George groaned. "Everyone thinks I'm the Phantom. Even you guys doubt me a little bit. Come on, admit it."

Alex, Julianna, and Chris looked **sheepishly** at the ground.

"Nah," Chris said finally. "Not really."

"You'd never do something like this," Julianna added.

"Not on purpose," Alex said. "And the Phantom is definitely doing this on purpose."

George smiled. It was nice to know his friends were still in his corner. "But if Principal McKeon cancels that parade, they're gonna **run me out of town**."

"You're exaggerating," Alex said.

"Okay, run me out of *school*," George corrected himself. "I gotta find a way to stop these pranks. And fast."

Chapter 8

Later that afternoon, George sat
at his desk trying to do his homework.
But it was **impossible** to concentrate
on multiplying fractions when he knew
practically the whole school was blaming
him for the pranks.

George had to **solve this mystery**.
Otherwise everyone would hate him.
Quickly he picked up his pencil and began
writing on a blank page in his notebook.

CLUES

  1) The Phantom is strong enough
     to turn over desks.

That means he can't be a little kid,
George thought to himself.

  2) The Phantom uses cutout
     letters so no one will
     recognize his handwriting.

  3) The Phantom can move around
     the school without being
     noticed.

  4) The Phantom gets to school
     early so he can set up some
     pranks before anyone else
     gets there.

George looked at that last clue and
started to laugh, remembering the **rubber
nose** on the Edith B. Sugarman statue,
and the rubber mask over the skeleton's
head. Those two pranks were hilarious.

  5) The Phantom is a funny guy.

George crossed out that clue. It pointed **straight at him**. And that wasn't a good thing.

George frowned as he looked back at his notes. All he'd figured out was that the Phantom was **someone big**, someone who didn't want the kids to recognize his handwriting, and someone who got to school early. That could be any one of a hundred different people.

Grrr . . . things sure looked *ba-a-ad* for George!

But he wasn't going to give up. He just had to **think harder**. There had to be more clues somewhere. Maybe in the notes the Phantom had left.

Still, the more George thought about those notes, the more confused he got. They were just a bunch of creepy **gobbledygook** about keeping your eyes open for the next chapter, checking the contents of your food, or covering your tracks. And of course there was that *really* weird one that pointed out the fact that skeletons didn't have **appendixes or stomachs**.

If there were any clues there, George sure didn't see them. This was a bummer, because as the Phantom had warned, the days before the parade were definitely numbered!

It was too bad George wasn't a **detective** in one of his mystery books. They were always able to figure out the clues and catch the bad guys. Sometimes they got the guy to admit he was the criminal, and sometimes they caught him **red-handed**.

But George wasn't a detective in a book. He was just a kid. And this was real life. There was no way George was going to catch someone red-handed.

But then again, **maybe he could**.
George had just come up with a great
idea. And he couldn't wait to get to school
the next day to put it into action!

Chapter 9

George was feeling pretty confident as he walked into the school building the next morning. He had a plan to **catch the Phantom**. All he had to do was wait for . . .

"OKAY!" Coach Trainer shouted as he ran out of the gym. "**I've had enough!** No one messes with my basketballs!"

Yes! That was just what George had been waiting for.

"Coach Trainer, what's wrong?" Mrs. Kelly asked.

"What's wrong? What's wrong?" Coach Trainer repeated.

He gasped. "Just go **look at the gym!**"

A whole crowd of kids followed Coach Trainer and Mrs. Kelly to the gym. Principal McKeon was already standing there.

"Oh boy!" Alex said as they walked into the gym. **"This one's bad."**

George looked around. Someone had dumped all the basketballs onto the gym floor. And to make things worse, they'd put **Halloween wigs** on the balls, and drawn faces on them with something that looked like lipstick.

"There's another note," Max said.

"Yeah, right here, on the wall under the basket," Mike added.

"Let me read that!" Louie said, ripping **the note** off the door. He started to read. "'This is my best prank yet. So I'm giving myself a new title: Phantastic Phantom.'

"I think we should **call the police**," Louie said. "I bet those basketballs have George's fingerprints all over them."

Everyone looked at George. But this time George wasn't frowning. He wasn't even shaking his head no. He was *smiling*.

"You won't find my fingerprints on those basketballs," he told Louie. "But you will find **a clue** on the *real* Phantom's fingers."

"You mean the Phantastic Phantom's fingers," Mike corrected him. He shook his head. "That's hard to say," he added.

Louie rolled his eyes. "What are you talking about, George?" he demanded.

A murmur went through the crowd. The other kids in school were obviously wondering the same thing.

"**I set a trap** for the Phantom," George told the kids. "Right here in the gym."

"How could you know the Phantom was going to strike in the gym?" Louie demanded. "Unless of course you *are* the Phantom."

"I'm not," George insisted. "I just figured that the Phantom had already pranked the cafeteria, the nurse's office, the lobby, a classroom, and the hallway. **The only places left** were the library or the gym. So right before I left school yesterday, I sprinkled a **heat-sensitive powder** all over the balls in the gym, and some of the books in the library. You can't see it, but it's there. The powder is invisible—until it makes contact with the heat of human skin. Then it turns red."

"He's lying," Louie told the kids. "George isn't smart enough to come up with a powder like that."

"No, I'm not," George admitted. "**But Alex is.** He read about it in a science magazine."

Everyone turned and stared at Alex. But Alex didn't say a word. He was too busy staring at George.

"At this very moment, the real Phantom's fingers should be **bright red**," George continued.

Everyone looked around. No one moved.

No one except Principal McKeon and Mrs. Kelly, that is. They turned their hands over, and **stared at their fingers**.

"It was you two?" George asked, surprised.

"What are you talking about?" Louie demanded. "They're our principal and our teacher. And their fingers aren't red."

"**Of course not.** I never actually had

any heat-sensitive powder," George said proudly. "I don't even know if it exists. But I did know the real Phantom would look at his hands to see if they were really red. I just never thought grown-ups would do this kind of thing."

George paused and thought about **the list of clues** he had made the night before. "But it makes sense," he continued. "You guys are big enough to turn over desks, you had to hide your handwriting because we've all seen it on our tests and papers, and you get to school before any of us do, so you could move the skeleton to Nurse Cuttaway's office or put the nose on the statue in the lobby."

Mrs. Kelly smiled. "Pretending there was a magic powder was **a good trick**, George. You caught us red-handed." She looked at her bare hands. "Well, sort of, anyway."

Principal McKeon laughed. "That was pretty sneaky. And pretty smart."

"Thanks," George said. "But there is something I still can't figure out. What's your motive? In every book I've ever read, the criminal has **a motive**."

"You're right," Principal McKeon replied.

"And our motive was to get you excited about *reading* books," Mrs. Kelly explained. "*Mystery* books. Because next month is going to be **Mystery Book Month** at Edith B. Sugarman Elementary School."

"Mystery Book Month?" Louie repeated.

"Yes," Principal McKeon told him. "Every grade in the school will be reading mysteries during the month of November. Solving your own mystery seemed like a fun way to get the mystery **excitement** started."

"Books," George repeated. "I should have known. There were clues in every one of the Phantom's notes. Words. Chapter. Contents. Cover. Appendix. Paging. Numbered. Title. **Those are all things you find in books!**"

"Exactly!" Mrs. Kelly said. She gave George a big, gummy grin.

"But how were you able to set up some of the pranks without us knowing?" George asked. "Like the worm in Sage's lunch?"

"The whole faculty knew about the pranks," Principal McKeon told him. "**The lunch lady** put the rubber worm in the food. Mr. Coleman stuck the quarter to the floor."

"That makes sense," George said. "No one would **think twice** about seeing him in the hallway."

Louie turned to Coach Trainer. "You

93

let them draw on the basketballs?" he asked, surprised.

Coach Trainer nodded. "It washes off. And it was all for **a good cause**."

"But why would you say you were going to cancel the parade for something *you* did?" Julianna asked Principal McKeon.

"I never said I was going to cancel the parade," Principal McKeon corrected her. "I just said that *privileges* can be taken away. **You kids** were the ones who decided that the privilege to be taken away was the parade."

"Besides, we were pretty sure one of you would **figure out the mystery** before that would happen," Mrs. Kelly said. She smiled proudly at George.

"I *had* to figure it out," George said. "There was no other way to prove it wasn't me."

"That sure was good motivation, George," Principal McKeon said. Suddenly she sounded very stern. "It was very unfair for you to be accused of **a crime** without any proof. I was surprised that that even happened. I thought the kids in this school knew better than to make anyone a scapegoat. I think some of your classmates **need to apologize**. Not now. But privately."

This time there was no mistaking who Principal McKeon was talking about—she was staring right at Louie.

Still, George was pretty sure Louie wasn't ever going to apologize to him. Louie never apologized for anything.

"Anyway, I did promise that there would be consequences for people's actions," Principal McKeon continued.

George gulped. Consequences? Uh-oh. Usually he was at the receiving end of Principal McKeon's consequences. And that often meant a phone call home to his mother.

But this time, Principal McKeon was smiling at him. "George Brown showed amazing creativity in solving this mystery," the principal told the crowd of kids. "He should be rewarded for it. This year, George will lead our parade!"

"WHAT????" Louie shouted. "That's not fair! My costume is going to be incredibly creative. Wait until you see! It cost my dad a fortune!"

"Now, Louie, don't be so upset. Everyone will still see your costume," Mrs. Kelly assured him. "Just not at the front of the line."

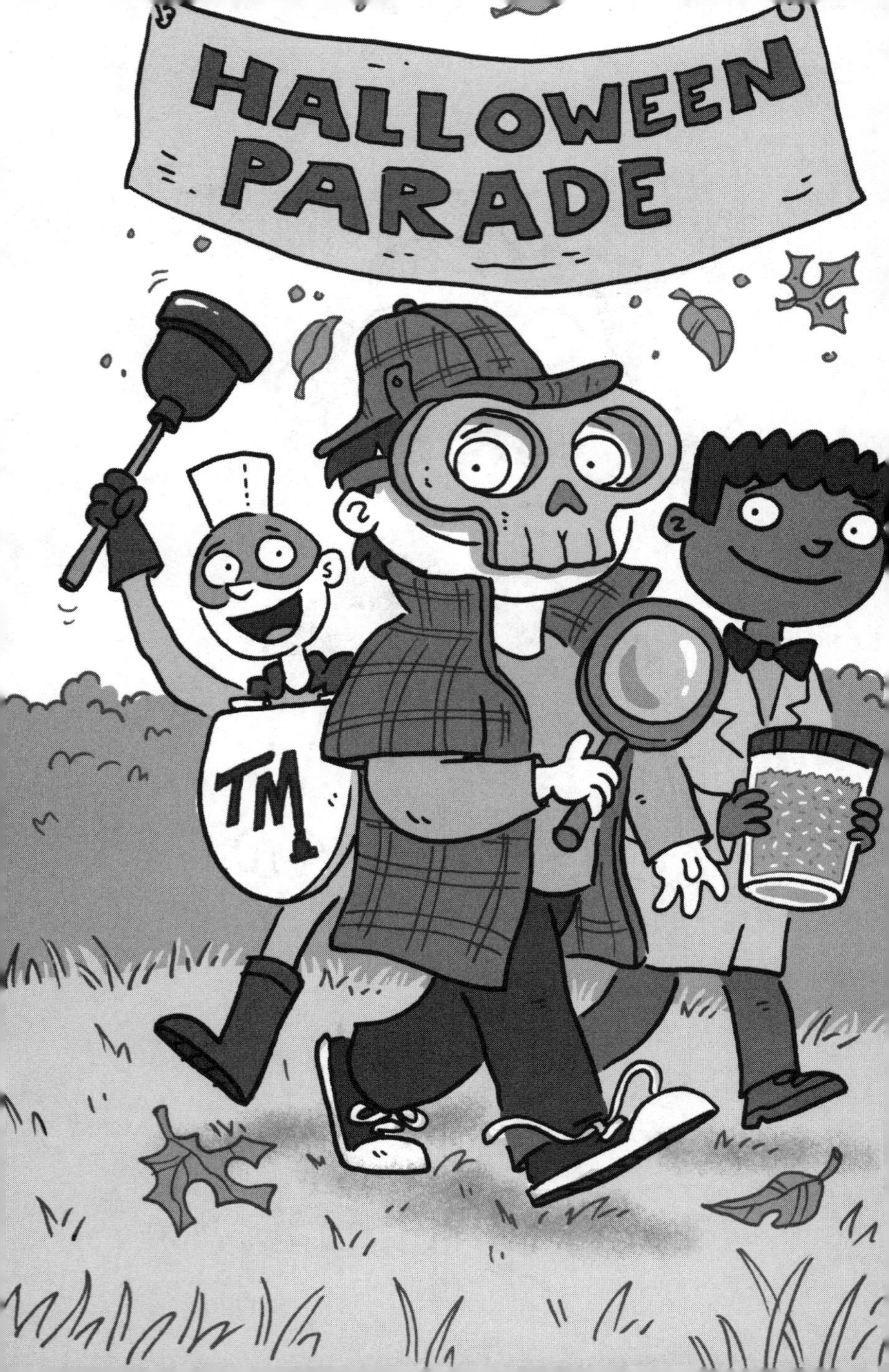
HALLOWEEN PARADE
TM

Chapter 10

"Wow! That's your best Toiletman costume yet," George complimented Chris as they all lined up for the Halloween parade.

"Thanks. My mom got me a **new toilet seat** to use as a shield," Chris replied happily. "And I also have my new plunger."

"Is that **real mold**?" Julianna asked Alex. At least that's what George thought she asked. It was hard to hear what she said from underneath the big football helmet she was wearing.

"No. My mom said it was too dangerous." Alex held up a jar filled with green and black dots. "This is rice with food coloring."

Just then Sage came running over. At least George thought it was Sage. Who else would come to school dressed as a pink-and-white **polka-dot ghost**?

"Georgie, who are you supposed to be?" she asked him.

She was probably batting her eyes up and down under the sheet. George was glad he couldn't see *that*.

George had on a skeleton mask. Over the mask he was wearing a baseball cap with brims in the front and the back. And he was carrying a giant magnifying glass.

"I'm **Sherlock Bones**," George said proudly. "Halloween detective."

Sage jumped up and down excitedly. "Ooo. Perfect," she squealed. "We're a Halloween couple after all."

Oh *brother*. "You're a polka-dot ghost,"

George said. "What does that have to do with Sherlock Bones?"

"You can call me Nancy *Boo*," Sage said. **"I'm a ghost detective."**

George rolled his eyes. Sage was a real pain. But he wasn't going to let her bother him. Not today. Not when he had the satisfaction of looking back at Louie, dressed as a giant pinball machine complete with **flashing lights**, at the very end of the line. All those lights just made it easier to see the jealous **scowl** on his face. Nope, nothing could ruin this day.

Grumble rumble. Uh-oh. Not the burp. Not now! Not

when he was about to lead the Halloween parade.

Grumble rumble.

George's tummy was definitely making some loud noises. But those weren't burp bubble noises. That was just George's stomach telling him **he was hungry**. So George reached into his pocket and pulled out a Nutty Nugget bar.

"I thought your mom said you couldn't have any of those until Halloween," Alex reminded him.

"My mom said this was **my reward** for solving the mystery of the Phantom," George told him. "Good thing, too. I need some Nutty Nugget energy."

Just then, music began to play through loudspeakers on the playground. "The foot bone's connected to the ankle bone. The ankle bone's connected to the leg bone . . ."

"Hey, they're playing my song!" said "Sherlock Bones" to his pals. "Come on. I have a Halloween parade to lead."

Then everyone—except Louie—**began to sing**.

"The leg bone's connected to the hip bone. The hip bone's connected to the backbone. Let's **shake** those Halloween bones!"

Spider Cider

Chapter 1

"Have you guys ever seen a pumpkin this big?" George asked his friends Alex, Julianna, and Chris one sunny Sunday afternoon in October. The kids were visiting Julianna's cousin's farm to find pumpkins for Halloween **jack-o'-lanterns**. Ever since the big parade at school, the kids hadn't been able to think of anything but Halloween! Now George had just found a pumpkin so huge it came up to his knees. It was the **biggest Halloween pumpkin in the patch**!

"It is really big," Julianna agreed. "But don't forget that you have to be able to carry it home."

"It's also lopsided," Alex pointed out. "And it's got **a green spot**."

"Yeah," George agreed. "I'd better keep looking. I know the perfect pumpkin is out here somewhere."

Chris reached down and picked up a medium-size pumpkin. "I've found mine," he said.

"Me too," Julianna said. She held up her pumpkin and spun it by the stem. "I can't wait to get home and **start carving**."

"It's really nice of your grandmother to let us carve the pumpkins at your house," Alex told her.

"Yeah," George agreed. "My mom hates when we carve pumpkins at our house. **Pumpkin guts** make a real mess."

"Grandma doesn't mind messes," Julianna told the boys. "She even baked her famous pumpkin pie for us."

"What's it famous for?" Alex asked.

Julianna shrugged. "Being eaten, I guess."

"Are your parents going to be there?" George asked.

Julianna frowned and shook her head. "They're in some mountain village near Russia, studying the eating and sleeping habits of people who live to be a hundred years old."

Julianna's parents were anthropologists. They were always **traveling around the world**, studying the way other people lived. While they were gone, Julianna's grandmother stayed with her and her older sister, Sasha.

"You mean they're just sitting there, watching **old people sleep**?" George asked her. "That sounds kind of boring." He picked up a pumpkin. Nope. This one had a brown spot near the bottom.

Better keep looking.

"It's not boring to them," Julianna replied. "They like watching people do things. I talked to my parents last night," Julianna continued. "They said they're bringing me back **a balalaika**."

"A bala-whatka?" George asked.

"Balalaika," Julianna repeated.

"It's sort of like a Russian guitar," Alex told him. "Except it's shaped like a triangle."

George looked at Alex with surprise. "How'd you know that?"

Alex shrugged. "I don't know. I must have read it in a book."

"Are you going to take balalaika lessons?" Chris asked Julianna.

"I don't think there are any balalaika teachers in Beaver Brook," Julianna replied. "I'll probably just put it on a shelf with the rest of the things my parents have brought back from their travels."

George reached down to pick up another pumpkin. And that's when he felt it. Something traveling inside *him*. **Something bing-bangy.** Something pling-plangy.

The magical super burp was back, and it was on the move! Already it had blasted its way out of his belly and sideswiped past **his spleen**. Now the bubbles were leaping off his liver and lunging toward his lungs. George shut his lips tight, and tried to keep the burp locked inside him.

But the burp was strong. The bubbles were ganging up on his gums. They were . . .

B-U-U-U-R-P!

Suddenly, George let out a burp. A *huge*

burp. A burp so big and so loud, it could drown out a band of balalaika players all the way over in Russia!

George opened his mouth and tried to say, "Excuse me." But that's not what came out. Instead he shouted, **"Feet don't fail me now!"** Then he began to race through the pumpkin patch at top speed.

"Dude, no!" Alex shouted.

Dude, *yes*! The magical super burp was free. And it wanted to play in the pumpkin patch!

George began leaping over giant pumpkins like an Olympic **track star** jumping hurdles.

"Don't go too far," Julianna called to him. "The **hayride truck** will be here soon to pick us up and bring us back."

Even if the super burp had heard Julianna, it wasn't about to listen to her.

It was too busy making George leap over pumpkins.

And then, suddenly, George's feet stopped running. His eyes spotted **a row of scarecrows** in the middle of the field. George's mouth smiled. His eyes danced.

His hands picked up a bowling ball–size pumpkin.

"Dude, don't . . . ," Alex shouted.

George's hand reached down toward the ground. His eyes stayed glued to the row of scarecrows. He reached his hand back. Aimed. And then . . .

WHEEEE! George rolled the bowling ball–size pumpkin right at the row of scarecrows. The pumpkin

slammed right into the middle scarecrow. The scarecrow teetered back and forth. It shook from side to side. And then . . .

Bam! The scarecrow fell to the ground. On its way down, it **knocked over** the scarecrow right beside it.

"It's a split!" George shouted out. He picked up another pumpkin and walked back to the foul line.

"George, don't!" Julianna called. "My cousin is going to be so mad."

But the super burp didn't care about Julianna's cousin. All it cared about was **bowling a spare** in the middle of a pumpkin patch.

George's hand reached down toward the ground. His eyes stayed glued to the row of scarecrows. He reached his hand back. Aimed. And then . . .

Pop. George felt something burst in the bottom of his belly. All the air rushed

out of him. **The super burp was gone.**
But George was still there. In the middle
of a bowling alley . . . er . . . in the middle
of a *pumpkin patch*.

His friends came
running over.

"George, what were you doing?" Julianna asked him.

George opened his mouth to say, "Bowling for scarecrows." And that's exactly what came out. "I'm sorry. I didn't mean to. I was just . . . um . . ." George didn't know how to finish that sentence. He didn't want to tell Julianna and Chris about the magic super burp. It was **embarrassing** enough that Alex knew about it.

"It's not a big deal," Alex assured Julianna. "We just have to stand them back up and stick the poles back in the ground. It won't take long."

George shot Alex a grateful smile. His best friend had saved him—again. But Alex couldn't save him forever. One day, the burp was going to burst out and cause some real trouble. **Trouble he couldn't get out of.**

George didn't know when and he didn't know how. He just knew it would happen. And that's what made it *really* scary.

Chapter 2

"Whoa! What are those?" George asked Julianna as they walked into her house later that afternoon. He pointed to a bunch of **scary-looking masks** hanging on the wall in the front hall.

"Mayan masks," Julianna said. "My parents brought them back from Mexico a couple weeks ago. They represent Mayan gods. They're made of jade."

George smiled and opened his eyes so wide they almost **bulged** out of his face. He looked a lot like one of the masks on the wall.

"This one looks **cross-eyed**," Alex said. He tried to cross his eyes, too. Then he shook his head. "That makes me dizzy."

There was always something new to see in Julianna's house. Walking through her house was like going through **a crowded maze** of weird—but cool—objects from all over the world. Every time George came over, he noticed something new. Like the bronze statue of a baboon with a baby on its back.

"Where's that from?" he asked Julianna.

"Africa, I think," Julianna said. "Just like that antelope carving next to it on the shelf."

George looked at the wall beside him. There was **a sword** hanging next to a tapestry that had sticks and cotton woven into it. There was a papier-mâché sculpture of an **old, wrinkled man** sitting on a shelf. And next to that was something that looked like a cross between an elephant's trunk and a flute.

"Where are you going to fit that balalaika your parents are bringing home?" George asked Julianna.

She shrugged. "I'm sure we'll be able to cram it in somewhere. We always do."

"Hey, look at us," Chris called out suddenly.

George turned around. Chris was standing on Alex's shoulders. They looked a little like the **totem pole** that was propped up in the corner.

"The wooden totem pole is from Alaska," Julianna told George. "The other totem pole is just made up of **some weirdoes** from Beaver Brook."

"Hey, who you calling a weirdo?" Alex said, crouching down to let Chris off of his shoulders.

Julianna laughed. "Anyone who would rather stand around in my hallway looking like a wooden totem pole than go in the kitchen and carve pumpkins is pretty weird."

"Can't argue with that," Alex agreed.

"Ooo, yeah, talk about **gooey guts**," George said, as he reached down deep into his pumpkin and pulled out a huge hunk of warm, slimy, stringy **pumpkin mush**.

"I'm glad pumpkin doesn't

taste like guts when you eat it," Chris said. "I wouldn't want to eat a **gooey guts pie**."

George grinned. That reminded him of a song they used to sing at one of his old schools. "School food's made of ooey, gooey gopher guts . . . ," he began to sing. "Mutilated monkey meat. Chopped-up canary's feet. All rolled up in all-purpose porpoise pus. And I forgot my spoon."

"Dude, that's gross," Alex said. He started to laugh.

"I'm glad we're not eating pie right now," Julianna added.

"Me too," Chris agreed. He pulled some ooey, gooey pumpkin guts out of his pumpkin. "Okay, I'm **ready to start** carving. My pumpkin's hollow."

Julianna handed him some paper and a few pins. "Cool. All you have to do is draw your jack-o'-lantern design on the paper. Then you pin the paper onto your pumpkin and use these pumpkin-carving tools to carve along the lines."

Julianna pointed to some small, sharp **carving knives** on the table. They were all different sizes and shapes. "But we gotta wait for my grandma to get here before we actually carve. She wants to supervise."

Chris started drawing right away. But George had no clue what he wanted his jack-o'-lantern to look like. Then he looked up on the kitchen wall. There was a metal sculpture with **pointy gold teeth** and whirly, swirly green metal eyes. Yes! That mask was the perfect inspiration for a jack-o'-lantern.

Then again, so was the middle face on the totem pole in the hallway. Or the

Mayan mask George had seen when they first walked in. Or the face that was painted on the **Egyptian mummy case** propped against the side of the refrigerator. Wow! There was so much to choose from!

The only things that decorated George's house were paintings of sunsets his grandmother had done in her art class, beaded fruit and silk flowers his mom had made at her craft shop, a lamp his dad had made from **a soda can** in his high-school shop class, and a bunch of family photographs. Bo-ring!

George wished his house was more like Julianna's. Because living in a house like this would make every day feel **like Halloween**!

127

Chapter 3

"You made *another* jack-o'-lantern?" George asked Chris as they arrived at school on Monday morning.

"Yup." Chris nodded. "I had **so much fun** at Julianna's that I decided to carve another one when I got home."

"But why'd you bring it to school?" Alex asked.

"I thought it would get our classroom in **the Halloween spirit**," Chris explained. "I carved Edith B. Sugarman's face into the pumpkin."

"That woman's face is so **creepy**," George said. "I don't know why they named our school after her."

"But it's the perfect face for a jack-o'-lantern!" Chris said.

Just then, Louie came rolling up to the boys on his wheelie sneakers. George **laughed**. *Speaking of faces that are perfect for jack-o'-lanterns . . . ,* he thought. But he didn't say it out loud. That wasn't the kind of thing a new improved George Brown would say. And George was really trying to be **new and improved**.

"Here," Louie said, shoving envelopes into George, Alex, and Chris's hands.

"You're all invited to my Halloween party Sunday night."

George looked at Louie curiously. Louie hated George. He had since the very day George had arrived in Beaver Brook. He hated him so much that for a month **he hadn't even called him by his name**. He'd just called him New Kid.

"My mom said I had to invite the whole class," Louie told the boys.

Oh. That explained it.

"And she said to tell you she'd be keeping her eye on you, George," Louie continued.

WHOOSH

George wasn't surprised. Louie's mom had seen George do some really **weird things**—like practically ruin Louie's birthday party at a water park. George **pinched people's butts** while they were floating in the lazy river in inner tubes. And then there was the time George had tried to ride the Rudolph the Red-Nosed Reindeer decoration on Louie's front lawn.

Of course, none of those things had been George's fault. It had all been the **magic super burp**. But there was no way George was telling Louie that. Louie thought George was weird enough as it was.

"It's going to be the best Halloween party ever," Louie told the boys. "We're going to have music and games, and **a piñata** filled with candy. Everyone's going to be talking about my party."

Just then, Max and Mike walked over. They stood on either side of Louie.

"I'm coming to **your party**, Louie," Mike said.

"I was just going to say that," Max told Mike.

"Yeah, well, I said it first," Mike told Max. He turned to Louie. "I bet I'm the first one to say I was coming, right?"

"Yep, you are," Louie told Mike.

"Well, I would have been first, if you hadn't **butted** in and said it before I did," Max told Mike.

George rolled his eyes. This was the dumbest conversation he'd ever heard.

Luckily, at just that moment, Julianna came walking over. Boy, was George happy to see her.

But Julianna **didn't look happy**. She was scowling. And she had her arms crossed over her chest.

"What's with you?" George asked her. Julianna shrugged. "I'm in a **bad mood**."

Louie handed her an invitation. "This will cheer you up," he said. "It's an invitation to my Halloween party Sunday night."

"Sunday's Halloween," Max said as if he'd just figured it out.

"**The perfect night** for a Halloween party," Mike said. "Good thinking, Louie."

Julianna shrugged and stuck the invitation in her backpack. "Thanks."

"You didn't even look at it," Louie told her. "It's an amazing invitation. There's a witch with **glow-in-the-dark**

eyes on the front."

"I'll look at it later," Julianna promised.

Louie frowned and pulled out some more envelopes. "I have to go give these to the people lucky enough to be invited to my party. I'm sure they'll be **more excited** than you are."

As Louie skated off, with Max and Mike trailing behind, George stared curiously at Julianna. "You look miserable," he told her.

"What happened?" Alex asked.

"My parents called from Russia last night," Julianna replied.

"That should make you happy," Chris said.

"Usually it does," Julianna agreed. "But this time it was awful. My mother said we had to **clean up the house**."

George looked at her strangely.

"That's not so bad," he said. "I'm always having to clean up stuff. Probably because **I'm always making messes**."

"Yeah," Chris said. "You should have heard my mom when I **spilled** all my paints. She was really mad. But then I cleaned it up and everything was okay again."

"Same thing happened when my last **science experiment exploded** in the kitchen," Alex told her. "We all have to clean up sometimes."

Julianna frowned. "It's not the cleaning that's so awful," she explained to the boys. "It's *why* I have to clean that's the problem. My parents said that my sister and I have to clean the house because some people are going to be **coming by** on Friday."

"So you have to clean for company?" Alex said. "That's no biggie."

"They're not company," Julianna told him. "These people are coming to see my house because **they might want to buy it**."

"What did you say when your parents told you that?" Alex asked.

"I didn't say anything, because they didn't tell *me*," Julianna said. "I overheard my grandma telling them that the house would be in **perfect shape** when the real estate agent came. That's how I know what's happening."

George gulped. Now he understood why Julianna looked so sad. It was the same look he got on his face whenever his dad told him they were **going to move**. He was willing to bet she had the same pit in her stomach, too. George's dad was in the army, so his family had moved around a lot. **Moving was the worst.** You had to say good-bye to all your friends.

This was the first time in a long time that George wasn't the one who was moving away. But that didn't make him feel any better. Having to say good-bye to Julianna was really **going to stink**. She was one of his best friends. And she was the best pitcher on the fourth-grade baseball team. The whole school needed her.

"We can't let this happen!" George exclaimed.

"I don't think there's any way to stop it," Julianna told him. "The people are coming Friday to look at the house."

"There's gotta be a way," George told her. "I don't know what it is, yet. But I'll think of something."

Chapter 4

"And, of course, we're going to **bob for apples**," Louie announced at the lunch table later that day. "And then there's the piñata I told you about. We're going to have a contest for the best costume, too. My costume is going to be incredible. You guys are lucky my mom said I can't win since it's my party. And my brother, Sam, is letting me use his iPod for the music, which is great because nobody has **cooler songs** on their iPod than Sam . . ."

George shook his head. He really couldn't listen to Louie blab on and on about his party anymore. He was too bummed about Julianna. She was sitting there, just staring at her lunch.

Every now and then, she would **poke** at her macaroni and cheese with her fork and sigh.

"Any ideas yet, George?" Chris asked.

"Not yet," George admitted. Then he looked over at Julianna and smiled. "But I'm not giving up."

"You're lucky, Julianna," Sage said.

Julianna stared at her. "Lucky?" she asked. "How can you say that?"

"Because Georgie is helping you," Sage said. She turned to George and **batted her eyelashes** up and down. " Georgie is really smart. He can solve anything."

George really hated when Sage called him Georgie. It was embarrassing. Sage was a real pain. She was also really wrong. This seemed to be the one problem George had **no clue how to solve**. The one problem besides his burp, that is!

"It stinks that your house is so cool," Alex said. "If there was something wrong with it, no one would want to buy it."

"That's true," Chris agreed. "It's too bad you don't have **termites** or a leaky roof."

"I wouldn't want to live in a house with termites," Sage said. "Think about how creepy it would be sleeping in a house that's being **eaten by bugs**."

Suddenly, George's eyes lit up. "That's it!" he exclaimed.

"What's it?" Alex, Chris, Julianna, and Sage all asked him.

"I know how we're going to stop your parents from selling that house!" George said. "We're going to make your house **so creepy** no one will ever want to live there."

"You're not going to turn a bunch of termites loose, are you?" Julianna asked. "Because then even *I* wouldn't want to live there."

George shook his head. "Nope. No termites. We're gonna . . ."

"I don't believe you guys!" Louie interrupted angrily. "How can you talk about Julianna's house at a time like this?"

"A time like what?" Alex asked.

"A time when I'm about to throw the biggest, **best Halloween party ever!**" Louie exclaimed. "I've been telling you all about it. But not one of you was listening to me."

George couldn't argue with that. He hadn't heard much of what Louie had said.

"I listened," Max assured Louie.

"I heard every word you said."

"Me too," Mike agreed. "You told us we were gonna break open apples, and **bob for piñatas**, and—"

"That's not right," Max interrupted. "He said that there's gonna be a contest for the best apple. And we're going to **break-dance to music** and—"

"Break-dance?" Louie asked. "I didn't say anything about break dancing. I said break a piñata. And bob for apples."

"Oh right," Max said. "Sorry, Louie."

"Tell us again," Mike added. "I'll listen better this time."

George didn't hear the rest of Louie, Mike, and Max's conversation. He was thinking about something more important. There was a **plan hatching** in George's brain. He couldn't wait to get started on Operation Save Julianna's House!

Chapter 5

"I figure nobody would want to buy a haunted house," George told Julianna, Chris, and Alex as they sat on the steps outside the school at the end of the day. **"So, we're going to make your house haunted."**

Julianna gave him a funny look. "How?" she asked him. "It's not like you can go to the store and buy a ghost."

"*We're* going to be the ghosts," George explained.

"Oh, I get it," Alex said. "We're going to turn Julianna's house into the kind of haunted house you see **at a carnival**."

"Exactly," George said. "Creepy

noises, cobwebs, wind blowing even though the windows are closed . . ."

"We can use some of my remote-controlled toys," Alex added. "I could rig it up so something scary runs across the floor. Like **a rat**."

"And a black cat," George suggested. "It's bad luck if one of those crosses your path. No one will want to move into a house with bad luck."

"I could make **a spooky painting** with glow-in-the-dark paint," Chris added.

"Perfect," George said. "And considering how much creepy stuff is already in Julianna's house—"

"Hey!" Julianna interrupted.

"I didn't mean it like that," George explained. "The stuff in your house is **creepy-cool**. The stuff we do will be creepy-scary."

"Scary enough to frighten away the

people who want to **buy my house**?" Julianna asked.

"Yes," George replied. "We'll make sure of it."

"Check it out!" George exclaimed as he walked into the classroom the next morning. **"Skulls."** He picked up the small skeleton head that was sitting on his desk. It was a little bigger than his fist.

"They're made of sugar," Sage said as she examined the skull on her desk. **"Sweet like you, Georgie."**

George rolled his eyes. He really wished she would stop calling him that.

"What's this all about?" Mike asked, poking a skull.

"I have no idea," Max said. "Let's ask Louie."

Louie stared at his two friends. "Skeleton heads. It's about Halloween. *Duh*. I swear you two are just as empty-headed as these **sugary skulls**."

George laughed. That was actually a pretty funny one, even if it came from Louie.

"I know what these are for," Alex said. "We're celebrating the Mexican **Day of the Dead**."

"Very good, Alex," Mrs. Kelly said as she walked into the classroom.

The kids all stared at their teacher. She was dressed in a **witch's hat and cape**. In her hand she was carrying a broom.

"We're also celebrating Walpurgis Night," Mrs. Kelly explained. "Which is Witch Night in Germany. And Chinese Hungry Ghost Night. See how I placed those **pieces of bread** and a glass of water in front of a picture of some of my old relatives?"

The kids all stared at their teacher. George gulped. He wondered what was coming next. Usually when Mrs. Kelly started doing something this weird, it **involved dancing**. Mrs. Kelly loved to dance. George hated it.

"These are festive celebrations from around the world," Mrs. Kelly explained. "Even though not every country **celebrates** on October thirty-first like we do, all the holidays are very similar."

"So do we get to eat these candy skulls?" Max asked her.

"Well, you're going to decorate them first," Mrs. Kelly said. "I have **icing and all sorts of candies** you can use. I've laid everything out on the table in the back of the room."

George turned around. Sure enough there were small plastic bowls of icing and bowls of jelly beans, candy mints, licorice strings, Red Hots, and lemon drops just waiting for them. It looked like **a real life version** of the Candy Land game. He couldn't wait to dig his hands into all those sweets!

Mrs. Kelly held up a sugar skull she had already decorated. It was covered in candy and icing and looked delicious!

"Let's get to it!" George exclaimed excitedly.

"We will," Mrs. Kelly said. "But first,

we're going to play **snap apple**."

"What's that?" Sage asked.

"It's a Halloween game from Ireland, the place where Halloween began," Mrs. Kelly explained as she pulled a bag of apples out from under her desk. "These apples are all attached to strings. I'm going to hang the apples in the doorway. Each of you will get a chance to try to **grab an apple in your mouth**—without using your hands."

"That's kind of like bobbing for apples **without water**," Louie said.

"Exactly," Mrs. Kelly replied.

"At my party, we're going to do it

with water," Louie said.

"I think you'll like grabbing the apples in your mouth this way, Louie," Mrs. Kelly assured him. "It's fun!"

Louie didn't look so sure.

At the moment, George wasn't having too much fun, either. It was hard to have fun when you felt something bubbly bouncing in your belly.

Bing-bong. Ping-pong. The burp was back. And it was **going wild** trying to make its way out of George's belly. Already the bubbles were itching his intestines and creeping up his colon.

Zing-zang! Cling-clang! The bubbles were moving fast. **George had to stop them**. He had to force that super burp back down before it exploded right out of him.

So George did the only thing he could think of. He leaped up out of his seat and started **swirling around and around**, trying to force those bubbles down to his feet the same way **toilet water** swirled down the drain when you flushed!

"George, what are you doing?" Mrs. Kelly asked. "Please sit down."

George wanted to sit down. **He really did.** But he couldn't. Because if he stopped swirling, the bubbles would move back up through his body and out of his mouth. And if that burp got loose, there was no telling what it might do!

Whirl. Swirl. Twirl. The bubbles started going down the drain!

"George Brown, sit down!" Mrs. Kelly shouted. "This is no time for crazy dancing." The teacher stopped and shook her head. "I can't believe I just said that," she remarked.

But George **kept spinning**. The bubbles hit his hips. They threaded around his thighs. They knocked against his knees. Down, down, down they went. It was working! George twirled faster and faster and faster. *Clank. Clunk.* The bubbles kicked at his calves.

Spin. Spin. Spin. George twirled toward the back of the room. Past Julianna's desk. Past Sage's desk.

"Look at Georgie go!" Sage squealed.

Spin. Spin. Spin. **He whirled** through the reading corner.

Spin. Spin. Spin. He swirled over

toward the bowls of icing and candy Mrs. Kelly had set up in the back of the room.

Spin. Spin . . . *Pop!* Suddenly, George felt something burst in the bottom of his belly. He'd done it! He'd squelched the belch!

Whoa . . .

But George couldn't celebrate his victory. **The room was still spinning**, even though George wasn't moving at all.

"I'm so dizzy," George groaned.

The room kept spinning. George took a step. His body swayed back and forth.

Slam! George lost his balance, and fell face-first—right into a big bowl of **gooey blue icing**. *Uh-oh.*

"George!" Mrs. Kelly exclaimed.

George picked up his blue head, and looked at his teacher. "I'm sorry," he said.

"Georgie, you look like a sugar skull." Sage giggled. **"I could just eat you up."**

George rolled his eyes and groaned.

"We can't eat any of the blue icing now," Louie complained. "It's got **George germs** in it."

"It's okay, Louie," Mrs. Kelly assured him. "We have lots of other colors." Then she gave George a stern look.

"Go wash your face. And then you can come back, and **sit at your desk**, and study this week's spelling list."

"But what about making a sugar

skull?" George asked. "Don't I get to . . ."

"I'm sorry, George," Mrs. Kelly interrupted him. "After what just happened, I don't think you deserve to be part of the **sugar-skull fun**. I know you're excited about Halloween, but this was not the time or place to go crazy."

George frowned. It wasn't his fault. But he couldn't tell his teacher that. He'd just have to suffer the consequences. Again.

Chapter 6

"I've rigged up a remote-controlled **black cat** that can cross right in the path of the people who are thinking about buying your house," Alex told Julianna later that day as the kids sat at their lunch table in the cafeteria. "And two remote-controlled rats. That'll scare them!"

George flicked **a piece of hardened blue icing out of his nose** and rubbed it on his napkin. "I have lots of dust bunnies under my bed," George added. "We can hang them from some of the shelves in the house. Haunted houses always have **lots of dust** around."

"I've got dust bunnies, too," Chris said. "I'll bring them over. My mom will be glad to get rid of them. And I'm working hard on my painting," he continued. "I'm drawing the eyes so it seems like they **follow you** around the room. I learned how to do it from an art book my dad gave me."

"*Georgie*, your idea is brilliant," Sage said. She batted her eyelashes up and down. "*You're* brilliant."

"STOP! STOP! STOP!" Louie shouted suddenly.

George stared at him. He couldn't believe it. He'd been wanting to tell Sage to stop calling him Georgie. And here, **Louie had just done it for him**.

"Stop talking about Julianna's house," Louie continued.

Or maybe not.

"There's something much more important happening," Louie continued.

"What could be **more important** than my family moving?" Julianna wanted to know.

"My party," Louie said. He sounded as if he couldn't believe she was even asking. "Halloween is almost here, and no one is even thinking about what costume to wear to my party. And you're **going to be sorry**, because the prizes my mom is getting for the costume contest are really, really expensive!"

"I'm thinking about my costume,"

Max assured Louie. "It's the only thing on my mind."

"Me too," Mike said. "I've got lots of ideas. I just **can't remember** any of them right now."

Louie grinned. "Well, you guys are just lucky I can't win the costume contest," he told everyone. "Because my **space-alien-creature** costume is going to be the coolest. It's coming all the way from Hollywood. One of my dad's clients knew a guy whose uncle was the assistant costume designer on a **scary movie**. He's sending me a costume from his latest film—*Slimy Space Salamanders from Saturn*. I know none of you can beat that, but I'm sure you can come up with something that's pretty good—if you start thinking about it now!"

"We'll get right on it," George

told Louie. "As soon as we stop these people from buying Julianna's house on Friday."

Louie shook his head. "Your stupid idea will never work. Nobody believes in haunted houses anymore. **And nobody believes in ghosts, either.**"

"Sure they do," Julianna shot back. "My house is filled with masks that people from all around the world have made to scare away **evil spirits**, including ghosts."

"None of those were made in Beaver Brook," Louie told her. "Because no one in Beaver Brook believes in evil spirits."

George opened his mouth to argue with Louie. But then he stopped. Unfortunately, Louie had a point. And to make things worse, there was a point that even Louie hadn't brought up. What if the masks thought the made-up ghosts were real? Would they do something to **scare the fake ghosts away**?

Oh no. No way. George was not going to start thinking about that. Not now. This wasn't the time to think **bad thoughts**.

Unless of course you were Louie. He didn't seem to have any trouble thinking bad thoughts. **"Face it, Julianna,"** Louie continued. "You're moving. But there's a bright side."

Julianna scowled angrily and glared at him. "What bright side?" she demanded.

"Your last memory of Beaver Brook will be my party," Louie told her. "The best party ever. Of course it can't be your going-away party, because it's my Halloween party. But still, you will always remember it because of its **awesomeness**."

"Wrong, Louie," George told him.

"Are you saying my party won't be awesome?" Louie demanded angrily.

"No. I'm saying it won't be Julianna's last party in Beaver Brook," George told him. "Because Julianna isn't going anywhere. Her parents aren't going to sell her house. **Our plan is going to work.**"

"I sure hope so," Julianna told him. "My whole life depends on it."

Chapter 7

"Okay, we have everything we need," George told Julianna as they walked onto her front porch. Chris, Sage, and Alex followed close behind. "You're sure your grandma **won't be here** while we're setting up?"

"Positive," Julianna assured him. "She plays cards at the Community Center every Friday. Sasha is here, though. She'll help us."

"Your sister wants to help?" George was surprised. Sasha was in **eighth grade**. She usually didn't want to have anything to do with fourth-graders. In fact, George had actually only met her

twice the whole time he'd been living in Beaver Brook.

"She's not sure our plan will work," Julianna said. "But she's willing to try anything **to keep us from moving**."

"*There* you are," Sasha said, opening the door. "What took you so long?"

"We get out of school after you do," Julianna reminded her.

"Well, you'd better get working," Sasha said. "The real estate agent is going to be here really soon."

"Where do you want these **squishy eyeballs**?" Sage asked Sasha. She pulled a plastic bag out of her backpack.

"How about in that clay bowl from Guatemala?" Sasha suggested, pointing to a bowl that looked like it had brown, blue, and white eyes already painted all over it.

Sage emptied her bag of **slimy**, wet eyeballs into the bowl.

"Yuck!" Julianna gasped. "They look real."

"Don't they?" Sage agreed. "They're just **peeled grapes**. But I used paint to draw colored irises in the middle of them. Do you like my eyeballs, Georgie?"

George looked down at the bowl of grape eyeballs. "Pretty cool," he had to admit.

"I'm dropping these **plastic spiders** into the glasses of apple cider," Chris told Julianna. "One sip and **they'll freak!**"

"Spider cider," George said with a laugh.

"I'm going to hide in the closet with my remote-controlled black cat," Alex said. "I'll let him out just in time for him to cross their paths."

"And I'll let the remote-controlled rats out when they come into the kitchen," George said. He grabbed a handful of **dust bunnies** and hung them off the side of a shelf.

"That looks really haunted house–like," Sasha complimented him.

"Thanks," George said proudly.

"Where do you want my painting?" Chris asked. He unfurled a painting of a **scary-looking man with creepy eyes**.

George moved to the left. The glow-in-the-dark eyes followed him.

George moved to the right. The glow-in-the-dark eyes followed him again.

"Wow!" George exclaimed. "That's super creepy."

"It gives me **goose bumps**," Sage said. She held out her arm to show George the little hairy bumps that had popped up all over her skin.

"Put the painting up in our room," Sasha told Chris. "We want them to think the upstairs is haunted, too."

Alex walked over and **attached something** to the light switch in the living room. Then he looked over at Julianna and George. "That should do it," he told them. "Give it a try."

Julianna clapped her hands. The lights in the living room **flickered** on and off. "Perfect," she told Alex.

George threw another pile of dust bunnies onto the totem pole. **"Aaachooo!"** he sneezed. "That one was especially dusty."

"I sure hope this works," Julianna said.

Just then, the doorbell rang.

"Is that them?" George asked nervously. He started heading toward his **hiding place** in the cupboard.

"It can't be. They're not supposed to come for another half hour. That's when grandma said she would be back with the '*company*,'" Sasha said, making imaginary quotation marks in the air. "I can't believe she's calling them that."

"She doesn't know we know about Mom and Dad selling the house," Julianna reminded her sister. She walked to the door and looked through the peephole. "It's Louie," she told the other kids.

"What's he doing here?" George wondered.

"Probably reminding us to start making our costumes," Alex said. "Like we have time for that."

Julianna opened the door. "Hi, Louie," she said.

"Hi, Julianna. How's your house haunting coming?"

"Really, really great," George answered. "Why? Are you here to help?"

Louie shook his head. "Nope. I'm here to watch you **mess up**," he said with a smirk.

Julianna's mouth dropped open. She looked like she might cry. Or scream.

"Why would you say that?" George demanded. "Don't you know that if we fail, she moves?"

Louie shrugged. "**She's gonna move anyway.** Which is a bummer. But this plan of yours is going to be a disaster. And my film crew is going to record it all for my next *Life with Louie* webcast."

Film crew? George looked out the door. Sure enough, there were Max and Mike. They were **fighting** over which of them got to hold the camera.

"Louie said I could be the cameraman," Max said.

"He told me the same thing," Mike said. "And I'm holding the camera."

Louie smiled. "You guys can take turns," he suggested. "I'm sure George will do **lots of stupid stuff**. Enough for both of you to film for my webcast."

George rolled his eyes. This was not about Louie and his webcast. And it wasn't about George, either. It was about making sure no one bought Julianna's house. Besides, he was **too busy** making sure the house looked really scary to pay much attention to Louie. The grape eyeballs, the dust bunnies, and the remote-controlled rats were definitely **spooking up the place**.

Unfortunately, there was something even more spooky going on inside George. Bubbles in the belly. Lots of them.

Bing-bong. Ping-pong. The bubbles were already hip-hopping on George's heart and leaping onto his lungs.

George couldn't risk having the burp

mess up things now. Quickly, he ran
toward the back door and out into the
yard.

Alex saw George whiz by. He ran after
him. "Dude, not again!" Alex exclaimed.

Yes again. The bubbles were partying
on his arteries, and veering from his
veins. And then . . .

George let out **a giant burp**. A burp
so strong and so loud, it made the dust
bunnies hide under the table.

"Oh no!" Alex cried out.

Oh yes! The burp was out. And it
wasn't afraid of any haunted house.

"I gotta get you out of here before
you mess everything up!" Alex said. He

grabbed George and began to drag him to the front yard.

But the magical super burp didn't want to get out of there. **It wanted to play.**

George wrestled himself free of Alex's grip. He ran straight back toward the house. But along the way, he got all tangled up in some **white sheets** hanging on the line.

Now George couldn't see anything. Even magical super burps can't see through thick sheets.

But George's legs **didn't care** if his eyes couldn't see. They just kept running, right toward the house.

Bam! Slam! George banged into the back of the house.

Ouch! That hurt. But George's feet kept running. He raced through the open kitchen door and into Julianna's hallway.

"Whoa! What is that?!" Louie shouted. **"It's a ghost!"**

George wanted to laugh in Louie's face. Mr. I-Don't-Believe-in-Haunted-Houses sure sounded scared.

But the burp didn't feel like laughing. **The burp felt like running.** So George ran. And as he did, the white sheet brushed against some shelves. Dust bunnies flew up in the air.

Cough! Cough! Cough! "I'm allergic to dust," Louie said. *Cough! Cough!*

"Here, have some apple cider," Sasha told him.

Louie took the **apple cider**. He started to drink.

George was still wrapped in the sheet. He wanted to pull it off so he could see. But the burp wouldn't let him.

Slam! George bumped into Louie.

Splash! Cider flew out of the glass. So

did the plastic spider in the cider.

"Aaaahhhh!" Louie shouted. **"I hate spiders."**

George's legs kept running. *Whee!* He slid across the wet floor.

Bam! Slam! He knocked the bowl of cold, wet spooky eyeballs off the shelf.

"Aaaaahhhhh! **Eyeballs with no face** around them!" Louie shouted. "I'm getting out of here!"

Whoosh! Suddenly George felt something go pop in the bottom of his belly. The air just rushed right out of him. **The super burp was gone.** But George was still there. With a sheet on his head, surrounded by painted grapes and spider cider.

George lifted the sheet off his head and opened his mouth to say, "Sorry about that, Louie." And that's exactly what came out.

But Louie wasn't around to hear George's apology. He had already run out the door, with Max and Mike right behind him, filming everything.

George and his friends raced to the

door. They got there just in time to see **a woman with a clipboard** getting out of the front seat of a car. Then a man and a woman climbed out of the backseat.

A moment later, Julianna's grandmother pulled up right behind them.

"I'm sure you're going to love this house," George heard the real estate agent say. "It's . . ."

"Don't go in!" Louie interrupted, shouting at the real estate agent and the buyers. "You don't want to live there. That place is haunted!"

Chapter 8

"Julianna! Sasha!" the girls' grandmother shouted as she stormed into the house. **"What is going on here?"**

"Um . . . well . . . ," Julianna stammered.

"We . . . I mean *Julianna's* friends . . . ," Sasha began.

George frowned. Leave it to Sasha to **blame it all** on the fourth-graders.

Julianna's grandmother looked at Alex, George, and Sage. Then she looked up to see Chris coming down the stairs. "This was not the best day for a playdate," she told Julianna. "I told you we were having company."

"It wasn't a playdate exactly . . . ," Julianna began. "We were . . ."

"And what is with all this dust?" her grandmother interrupted. "I asked you to clean up. Why would you **make this place messier**?"

"Because we don't want to move," Julianna told her. "I know that's why these people are here. I heard you talking to Mom and Dad about it!"

"But why *wouldn't* you want to move to a bigger house?" her grandmother asked her.

George couldn't believe it. Julianna's grandmother sounded **so confused**. But why would she be? No kid would want to move away from his friends and his school.

"Because our whole lives are in Beaver Brook," Sasha told her grandmother. "I don't want to start over."

"But you wouldn't have to start over," Sasha's grandmother said. "You're only moving **a few blocks away**. You'll still be in Beaver Brook. You'll just have more room. Which you definitely need with all the junk your parents collect."

"Oh," Sasha said. "We didn't hear you say anything about that part. And Mom and Dad didn't tell us anything."

"Your parents weren't sure that they would be able to afford the bigger house, and they didn't want to get you excited," her grandmother explained. "But **they found one**. And the good news is, in the new house you each get your own room!"

Julianna smiled at the real estate agent and the people who were looking to buy her house. **"This is a really great house,"** she told them. "It looks a lot nicer without the dust and green grape eyeballs lying around. We just wanted

to make the place look haunted so you
wouldn't buy it, and we could stay."

"Beaver Brook is a great town," George added.

"Yeah," Chris agreed. "You can't judge us by that kid you met **running away**. Louie's not . . . he's not . . ."

"He's not like anyone else you'll ever meet anywhere," George said, finishing Chris's thought.

"I have a feeling Beaver Brook is a wonderful place," said the woman who was thinking about buying the house. "Otherwise why would you kids go to **so much trouble** to make sure your friend stayed here?"

George smiled. "Exactly."

Chapter 9

"Nice wig," Louie joked as he spotted Alex at his party on Halloween night.

"It's supposed to be messy," Alex told him. "I'm dressed as Albert Einstein. He was the smartest scientist ever. He was **too busy thinking** to brush his hair."

Louie didn't answer. He just turned to Chris. "You're dressed like Toiletman *again*?" he asked. "You wore that same costume in the school Halloween parade. You could have at least come up with something new for tonight."

"This time I have an **orange-and-black Halloween plunger**," Chris said. "And I'm carrying *four*-ply toilet paper."

Louie looked at Julianna. "Where'd you get that thing?" he asked, staring at the **big blue-and-green feathered eye mask** she was wearing.

"My parents brought it back from Brazil," Julianna said. "My mother wore it during a Carnival festival they went to down there."

George thought that was pretty cool. But he guessed Louie didn't, because he yawned and turned his attention to George.

"You're a mummy," Louie said, noting the **white bandages** that were wrapped all around George's head and body. "Not real original."

"It's a classic costume," George insisted. Then he looked at Louie's bright green jumpsuit and his antenna headband. "What are you supposed to be? **A giant glow-in-the-dark cockroach?**"

Louie's eyes got small and mean—
which made him look even more
like a cockroach. **"I'm a
space salamander,"** he
told George. "You know
that."

George grinned as
Louie stormed off. He
loved making Louie angry.

"You want to go check out
the piñata?" Alex said, pointing
to the giant **papier-mâché
pumpkin** that was hanging
from a tree in the middle of the yard.

George nodded and followed Alex and
the other kids walking over to take a look
at the piñata. As he walked, he scratched
at his arm. The bandages his mom had
wrapped him in were way too tight. But
George was dressed as a mummy. And
mummies never slipped out of their

bandages. So it was probably a good thing that the bandages were so tight.

"Oh, Georgie," Sage shouted as she came running over. "Look at us. **We're the perfect couple.**"

George looked at Sage. She was wearing a crown with a snake on it, and lots of dark black pencil around her eyes. "What are you supposed to be?" he asked her.

"Cleopatra," Sage said. She blinked her eyelashes up and down. "Queen of Egypt. You know, where mummies come from. You and I are both from ancient Egypt. We should probably **stick together** all night." George shook his head. No way. Not happening.

"George Brown, there you are," Mrs. Farley said as she came running over. "I've been looking for you."

"H-h-hello, Mrs. Farley," George said.

"I'm keeping my **eyes on you**," she told George. "This is Louie's party. Nothing funny is going to happen. You got it?"

George nodded. Louie's mom had *that* right. From the looks of things, nothing funny—or even *fun*—was going to happen here. Everyone was just sort of **standing around staring at one another**, while Louie's brother, Sam, played music.

"We're going to bob for apples now," Louie's mother announced. "**Loo Loo Poo**, you'll go first!"

George burst out laughing. *Loo Loo Poo*. It got him every time.

Louie's mother shot George a look. George stopped laughing. He'd almost forgotten. Nothing could be funny at Louie's party.

But as Louie **stuck his head** into a big vat of ice water and apples, George felt something funny happen. Not *ha-ha* funny. More like *uh-oh* funny. The magical super burp was back! Already the bubbles were bouncing around in George's belly, climbing up his colon, and invading his intestines.

Oh no! Not here! Not with Louie's mom watching George's every move!

But the burp didn't care who was watching. It wanted to have Halloween fun! The bubbles ricocheted off George's ribs. They trampled up his trachea. And then . . .

B-U-U-U-R-P!

George let out a burp so powerful, and so strong, it could be heard by real aliens up in space!

"George!" Mrs. Farley shouted. "What

do you say when you burp?"

George knew he was *supposed* to say, "Excuse me." He *wanted* to say, "Excuse me." But when he opened his mouth, all that came out was: **"It's T.P. time!"**

George's hands reached out and grabbed the toilet-paper rolls from Chris's costume and started throwing them at the trees in the yard.

"George, don't!" Chris shouted. "That's four-ply. It's **expensive**."

"Dude, we gotta get you out of here," Alex added.

But the burp wasn't going anywhere. Not until there was toilet paper wrapped over the branches of every tree in Louie's yard!

"Mom!" Louie shouted. "He's ruining my party . . . again!"

Louie's mother glared at George. **"You need to stop teepee-ing my yard—**

right now!" she warned.

George looked down. There was no more toilet paper. Only cardboard rolls. That meant the burp would have to stop spreading toilet paper around the yard.

But it didn't mean the burp would have to stop having fun. Before George knew what was happening, his hands picked up **a big stick**. His legs ran straight for the piñata. There was nothing he could do to stop them. And then . . .

Bam! George slammed the big stick into Louie's pumpkin piñata. Candy exploded all over the yard. **Kids dive-bombed** to the ground, scooping up candy.

"MOM!" Louie shouted. "*I* was supposed to break the piñata."

"George Brown, **what have you done**?" Louie's mother shouted.

Pop. Just then, George felt something burst right in the bottom of his belly. The air rushed right out of him.

The super burp was gone. But George was still there, surrounded by **candy and toilet paper**. He opened his mouth to say, "I'm sorry." And that's exactly what came out.

"I think it's time you leave," Mrs. Farley told him.

George didn't argue. He was thinking the same thing. He started to walk away.

"Wait up, dude," Alex said. "I'll go with you."

"Me too," Julianna said. "I'd rather trick-or-treat, anyway."

"Yeah, **trick-or-treating is the best part of Halloween**," Chris agreed.

George smiled at his friends. Chris was wrong about that. Trick-or-treating wasn't the best part of Halloween. Being with your friends was.

But **getting free candy** wasn't too bad, either!

"Come on, you guys!" George told his friends. "Let's get moving. There's a whole town's worth of candy waiting for us out there. And I can't wait to **sink my teeth** into it!"

About the Author

Nancy Krulik is the author of more than 150 books for children and young adults including three *New York Times* Best Sellers and the popular Katie Kazoo, Switcheroo books. She lives in New York City with her family, and many of George Brown's escapades are based on things her own kids have done. (No one delivers a good burp quite like Nancy's son, Ian!) Nancy's favorite thing to do is laugh, which comes in pretty handy when you're trying to write funny books!

About the Illustrator

Aaron Blecha was raised by a school of giant squid in Wisconsin and now lives with his family by the south English seaside. He works as an artist designing funny characters and illustrating humorous books, including the one you're holding. You can enjoy more of his weird creations at www.monstersquid.com.